Breathing Fire

Breathing Fire

Sarah Yi-Mei Tsiang

orca soundings

ORCA BOOK PUBLISHERS

Library and Archives Canada Cataloguing in Publication

Tsiang, Sarah, 1978-, author
Breathing fire / Sarah Yi-Mei Tsiang.
(Orca soundings)

Issued in print and electronic formats.
ISBN 978-1-4598-0566-8 (bound).--ISBN 978-1-4598-0565-1 (pbk.).--
ISBN 978-1-4598-0567-5 (pdf).--ISBN 978-1-4598-0568-2 (epub)

I. Title. II. Series: Orca soundings
PS8639.S583B74 2014   jc813'.6   C2013-906722-1
C2013-906723-x

First published in the United States, 2014
Library of Congress Control Number: 2013951368

Summary: Running away from her foster home, Ally finds herself on the busking
circuit, performing as a juggler and fire breather.

*Orca Book Publishers is dedicated to preserving the environment and has
printed this book on Forest Stewardship Council® certified paper.*

Orca Book Publishers gratefully acknowledges the support for its publishing
programs provided by the following agencies: the Government of Canada through
the Canada Book Fund and the Canada Council for the Arts,
and the Province of British Columbia through the BC Arts Council
and the Book Publishing Tax Credit.

Cover image by Getty Images

ORCA BOOK PUBLISHERS
PO Box 5626, Stn. B
Victoria, BC Canada
V8R 6S4

ORCA BOOK PUBLISHERS
PO Box 468
Custer, WA USA
98240-0468

www.orcabook.com
Printed and bound in Canada.

17 16 15 14 • 4 3 2 1

For Harriet and John,
Kendra and Matt:
my found family

Chapter One

A kid beside me, Bruce, tortures flies as Mr. Getty drones on about algebra. The flies spend all day ramming into the window and then dropping stupidly onto the metal sill. Maybe they're so desperate because they've been trapped inside this math class for most of their lives. Bruce plucks the wing off a fat one, and the fly spins, like a drunk winding up for a punch. I hit Bruce lightly on the arm.

"Stop it."

Bruce looks at me and rips off the other wing.

The principal opens the door. "Mr. Getty?"

As soon as they leave the room, everyone relaxes and starts chatting. I reopen the book in my desk.

Mr. Getty steps back into the room, and everyone stops. His eyes are red, and his mouth is set in a grim line. It looks like he's about to cry.

"Ally."

Everybody turns to look at me. My mouth opens and closes. I stand and shut my book. Outside the classroom, Principal Hearn puts an arm around me and leads me down the hallway. "We have some bad news for you, Ally."

Mom. What else could it be? I clamp my jaw shut because I don't want to ask.

I don't want to know. Suddenly, all I want to do is prolong this walk, this not-really-knowing, for the rest of my life. This moment of awfulness.

The school counselor is waiting for us—she's already seated by the principal's desk. I take a seat and cross my arms over my chest. I can't believe how cold it is in here.

"There's been an accident."

I nod to let him know I hear. I focus on the big picture behind him, an aerial view of the school. Each tiny student is a speck waving at the plane. I stare and stare until the picture wavers and becomes a blur of dark spots.

"Ally, your mom passed away this morning."

I knew it would happen. I knew it would. But today? This morning she seemed okay, dressed and up for work. Almost happy.

"How?"

"She was hit by a bus on the way to work. It all happened very quickly."

I want to wipe that sorry look off his face. I want my mom here so I can shake her. I want her here so I can have her hug me and tell me she won't try it again. I want her to wake up again like she did when I found her with the empty bottles of pills.

A bus. A fucking bus.

I try to figure out exactly what I was doing when my mom died. The coroner puts it at 9:23 AM. I think I was sitting down and opening my books in French class. I was supposed to have a dialogue using the verb *vouloir*.

I try it while I wait in the office of the social worker. Even French seems like a relief, something old and quaint from when my life was my own.

"*Je veux disparaître.*"

4

"Pardon?" The social worker looks up with a distracted, sad smile. She must practice it, I think, for all the tragic orphan cases like my own. I imagine her in her home, preparing for her day by making faces in the mirror. *Sad face. Tragic face. You'll-have-to-live-with-strangers face.*

"Look, I'm almost sixteen. I don't need foster care."

"Ally..." The social worker pauses and adjusts her facial expression to one of patient explanation. "It's the law. You're not old enough to take care of yourself. Normally, we would find a family to care for you, but in your situation..." She flips through the thin file one more time. "Are you sure you can't think of any relatives? Or maybe an adult friend that you and your mom were close to?"

I shrug. We both know it's impossible. Mom ran away from home because she was pregnant with me. It wasn't so much the pregnancy that my grandparents took exception to. It was more the fact that her baby would be a half-chink, a smear on their streak of white-only lineage. God forbid anything new be introduced to *that* gene puddle.

She changed her name, and I don't even know their last names. I don't want to either.

We arrive at the foster home after midnight. Everyone is in bed except for Darla, the foster "mom" who opens the door for us. She's short and round, wrapped in a brown bathrobe that is fraying at the edges. She exchanges a few words with the social worker and then looks me up and down.

"So. Ally. Is it okay if I carry one of your bags upstairs? You have a room to yourself tonight."

I grab the backpack that has my cash in it and hand her the duffel bag.

"Thanks."

I follow her upstairs and down a dark hallway. It's quiet, but I can hear the slight shuffling sounds of people shifting in their beds, the barely audible sighs of the sleeping. We go to the last bedroom. She opens the door to a neat and tidy room. It has two single beds in it and a scuffed desk.

Darla sets down the bag she's carried. "Are you good for tonight? Toothbrush, pajamas?"

I nod.

"There's a bathroom down the hall, first left. I'll wake you up in the morning, around eight."

When I finally crawl into bed and turn out the light, I'm surprised by the glow-in-the-dark stars that suddenly burn a greenish light. They are all over the ceiling, a stick-on galaxy.

Right above the bed, the stars are arranged into a glowing message: *Fuck U*, in slightly off-kilter writing.

The message makes me sad. It looks so small and pathetic. I turn onto my side and try closing my eyes, but I can't help seeing it, those green letters, the stupid kid-like message.

I kick off the covers and stand up. The stars are cool to the touch. I carefully unstick each one and rearrange them into a more or less random pattern of light. Then I lie back down. They are already starting to lose their glow. Watching them is like trying to focus on something from under deep water. I watch them until my eyes hurt, until they begin to well up with tears. Each one fades out, empty of light.

Chapter Two

When I open my eyes, I'm faced with a new room. It takes me a minute to work backward and figure out how I got here. Did we move again? I look up at the stupid plastic stars, and it comes back to me. I'm in a foster home. I'm in a foster home, and my mom is dead.

I should cry. I should really feel like crying. I dig my nails into my arm until the skin breaks open and little drops of blood well up. It stings, sharp and clear. At least some of me is still working.

My door opens with a bang, and a girl with bed head walks in.

"Shit. You're new?" She opens my closet and grabs a skirt and then looks down at me. She eyes my arm.

"Don't be a cutter. That's so cliché." She gestures toward the closet. "And I've got some of my stuff here, so keep your paws off."

She walks out with a little saunter. I already hate foster kids.

Darla knocks lightly on the open door. "Good, you're up. Come down for breakfast, would you? I've got lots of cereal. You don't have to go to school today. Your social worker will be picking you up."

The kitchen is dominated by a large Formica table and a bunch of ratty yellow chairs with food stains on the seats. In the middle of the table are boxes of Cheerios, Captain Crunch, Cocoa Puffs and some off-brand Raisin Bran. Darla points at an empty seat.

"Sit there, honey. Bowls on the counter and milk in the fridge. This is Rachel"—she points to the surly girl from earlier this morning—"and this here is Ben. Ben doesn't say much, do you, kiddo?"

Ben shakes his head. He looks about ten, with a mop of blond hair and a small head. Small everything—eyes, snub nose, thin little lips. A dribble of milk slides from the corner of his mouth.

"Darla says your mom croaked. That sucks." Rachel looks at me like she's waiting for me to bawl or start yelling.

"Yep."

There's a long silence as I eat my cereal and Rachel stares me down. Finally, she sighs and rolls her eyes at Darla.

"Awesome. We have another Ben."

"Oh shut it, Rachel. You'll be late for school." Darla reaches over and ruffles Ben's hair. "I'll take a quiet kid over a mouthy one any day of the week and twice on Sundays."

After Rachel and Ben are out of the house, I run up to my room and empty out all the cash from my backpack onto the thin comforter on the bed. The bills fall out, crumpled and dirty-looking. A quarter rolls off the bed and lands on the floor with a small ping. The pile of crumpled bills counts out to less than two hundred bucks. These few fives and twenties are all I have in the world, and I can stuff them all into my jeans pocket. I think about our shitty little apartment with the frayed secondhand couch and the sink that leaked and the mattress that smelled like piss. This is all Mom had in the world too.

I spend the day in the social worker's beat-up car. When we get to my apartment, the social worker sits on the couch and tells me to take my time. Mom's room is exactly the way I remember. It feels like it's been a thousand years since I was here instead of a night. Her nightgown is on the floor. There are some dirty socks sticking out of the hamper. Her bed is unmade, the sheets tossed into a loose pile at the bottom. I don't know what to take. I open up the closet and stand there like an idiot, my arms around an empty box. The social worker flips the TV on in the other room, and for a minute I let myself pretend that it's Mom in the kitchen, watching Dr. Oz while she cooks up a box of macaroni.

What is there to take? I walk around like a zombie and dump random things into a box. Her nightgown. Her Swatch.

Her runners. A plastic hair clip. I do it quickly, almost running. I don't want the social worker to come in and watch me decide whether to take a half-tube of mascara or the tacky solar dancing flower that Mom found in a thrift shop.

When we get back to the social worker's office, she types up the final few notes of my life.

"Ally, do you want a funeral for your mom? The province will pay for a basic one."

I have a sudden urge to punch the social worker in the face. You can tell that she's happy to be on her side of the desk. I want to yell at her, and I want to yell at Mom too. How do you live to be thirty-two and not have anything? No friends, no money, just a fucked-up daughter in foster care.

"I don't want anything. Just cremation." My mouth feels funny, like it's kind of numb.

"Ally, are you sure? I know this is a difficult time for you, and I don't want you to do something you'll regret."

"Who's going to go to her funeral? You?"

"I can if you want me to be there."

"Don't pretend you're my friend. You don't know anything about us. Just do your job."

Chapter Three

"I don't get why you don't have to go to school and I do." Rachel pouts dramatically as she stuffs her backpack with various books and makeup.

"It's the orphan prize. They're just giving me the marks I got so far. How much eye shadow do you need to take to one exam?"

"I want a sultry look. Also, I'm a traumatized, abandoned foster kid too. Shouldn't I get, like, half my exams off since my mom is in rehab?"

"No. Now stop bothering me. I have a lot of sleeping in to do."

Rachel leaves for school, and I wait until I hear the door slam for the last time this morning before I kick off my blankets. I'm so glad to be by myself during these last two weeks of the school year. I wander down to the kitchen and make myself a bologna sandwich. I put in three thick slices, even though the rule posted on the fridge says *One piece of meat per sandwich*. There are notes everywhere in the house. *10 minutes for showers*. *1/4 cup detergent MAX*. Darla wants to bring her husband and kids to Canada from some foreign country, so she's saving by buying bologna and raising foster kids.

After breakfast I grab my backpack and go for a walk. Mom's ashes are in the backpack, in a small cardboard box lined with plastic. I keep thinking that I'll find a place to put them—somewhere nice, somewhere she would want to be. When the social worker handed me the box, I almost thought it was some kind of sick joke. A cardboard box? But she shrugged and told me that since I had chosen not to go to the funeral home, there was no one to choose a proper urn. I guess I can go back sometime and get a metal one. Something classy. But I haven't.

I stop at the park and sit on the wooden bench. I take out the box. It's light but sturdy. I could just scatter everything here. There's a nice view of the river, and a little garden with flowers. I could mix the ashes into the garden.

The box is about the size of a fish bowl, and it's sealed with a solid line of tape. Part of me wants to take off the tape right now, just to peek inside. Is it like wood ashes, or are there maybe bits of Mom in it too? Like hair, or something that doesn't really burn well. A tooth, maybe.

"Hey, cutie. What have you got?"

There's a guy standing two feet away from me. He has on sweats and a hoodie. Graying hair. He's grinning like a pedo.

"My dead mother's ashes. Do you mind?" He turns and walks away without another word.

Mom would have liked that. One time we were riding the bus on the way to school. Mom spotted her then-boyfriend groping some other woman on the street. When the bus rolled to a stop, Mom poked her head out of the window and shouted, "You can have the no-good cheat if you want him, but he has two bucks in the bank and a small dick. Good luck!" After the bus rolled on, she turned to me and said, "Actually, I lied. He has at least ten dollars in the bank." You could tell everyone on the bus was trying to keep from laughing. Mom didn't believe in keeping jerks in her life, which was good, but I think sometimes that's why we moved so much. We were never moving *to* a new place, we were always moving *away* from where we were.

She was happy sometimes, and when she was up she was funny as hell. But it's hard to remember her like that. I can't even really picture what her face used to look like when she was happy. I can only really picture her when I remember the bad days. The days I would come home from school to find her in bed, all the curtains closed, her eyes red and raw. She could never really say why she got so sad. Maybe she felt like I do now. Maybe I can understand why she wanted to die.

Once I start crying, it's hard to stop. I hug the box tight to me and press my face to the cardboard. When I can finally breathe again, the cardboard is all splotchy from where it got wet. I wish I had something stronger to hold Mom together. I put the box back in my pack and wipe my eyes. I'll try to find a better place tomorrow.

Evenings at Darla's drag on for hours. She only has one TV with cable, and Darla gets the remote. She watches nothing but game shows and reality TV. She and Ben sit on the couch all night and stare at the tube. We're also not allowed out of the house after 8:00 PM. Rachel has argued so much with Darla over this that I don't even try. I can spot a lost cause.

Darla has one bookcase with some dusty VHS cassettes and a few romance novels (a blond shirtless man and a half-swooning girl with too much cleavage on each cover). I pick three cassettes and start juggling them. It's harder than juggling balls, especially since the cassettes keep slipping out of their sleeves, but it's still not much of a challenge. I miss the gymnastics gym, the high ceilings, the smell of chalk dust. The way a routine can focus your life to two minutes of impossible tricks. Rachel walks in and slams the door.

"She's such a bitch. I can't even take a walk because it's after eight." Rachel opens the door again and says loudly, "It's like living in a jail. Except the food is worse. Oh my god, who even has vhs anymore?"

"There's not much here, but if I have to watch *Big Brother 4* one more time I'm going to blow my brains out." I flip the tapes one more time and then pile them back on the shelf.

"Hey!" Rachel pulls out the tape I just put down. "*Titanic*. I know it's total cheese, but my mom and I used to watch it all the time. She was crazy over it for, like, a year and a half. I probably still know all the lines by heart. We can use the TV in the basement."

Rachel wasn't kidding when she said that she still knew every word of dialogue. We get to the end where the girl is hogging the raft.

I groan. "I can't believe you like this movie, Rachel. It's so weak."

"Shut up."

I give her a little kick. "You'd better get on the floor—there's not enough room on the couch for us both."

"There's totally enough room. Shut up."

"Exactly. There's totally enough room. On the floor and on the couch."

23

I give her another little kick in the rear.

We watch Leonardo start to sink, leaving nothing but bubbles on the surface.

Rachel looks down at her hands. "Yeah, well…it's kind of fitting, you know? Someone had to die. Sometimes you gotta save yourself."

I think of Mom walking in front of that bus. I don't know if she'd be Kate or Leo. Rachel sniffs, and I know she's thinking the same thing about her mom.

The weird thing about the way Mom died is I can't remember the last thing we said to each other. I've been trying to remember for the longest time, but it was probably just "See ya" when I walked out the door to go to school. She was making a sandwich when I left, and I think she just kind of waved with a mustardy butter knife in the air. I don't know if she ever said goodbye.

Movie deaths are better. You always know when someone is dying because they're gasping or shivering and looking pale and tragic. And you're always ready with a great line like, "I'll never let you go," and somehow everyone believes it.

Chapter Four

It's the first time I've ever snuck out of anywhere. Climbing out the window is actually pretty easy. Good on Darla for providing us with a rope ladder in case of fire. Or, you know, boredom.

Rachel hands me the screen, and I put it behind the headboard. It slips and lands on the hardwood floor with a loud thump.

"Ally," Rachel whispers, "could you not be a retard? For fuck's sake."

Rachel ties the rope ladder to the leg of the bed and swings the rest of it out the window. She scrambles on and disappears from sight.

I grab the top of the ladder and swing my feet out the window. The night is cool. I get a little shiver as I climb down. Rachel is putting on lipstick as she waits for me. She starts walking away the minute I touch my foot to the last rung.

"Hurry up. The bus will be there in five minutes."

On the bus, Rachel brings out Darla's makeup bag. She paws through it, trying to find an eye shadow that doesn't suck.

It was a city bus like this one that killed my mother. Or that Mom stepped out in front of.

I don't want to cry in front of Rachel, so I stare as hard as I can out the window, trying not to blink. I wonder if the passengers knew what they hit, or if it was just a crash and then nothing. I try to picture what it would be like to have been on that bus, maybe riding with a mom who isn't depressed. Who doesn't wake you up in the middle of the night to cry in your bed. Who remembers to pack you lunches. Who laughs on the phone with your grandmother, maybe while you learn to ride a bike with your dad. You're just sitting there, being all normal. Thinking about your day at school, and then *whump*, blood on the windshield and everyone screaming, grabbing their seats and trying to hold on. Except for you, because you can grab your mom, who has an arm pinning you, holding you for dear life.

"Jesus, Ally, get a grip," Rachel whispers in my ear, but she puts an arm around me and kind of half hugs, half nelsons me.

I wipe my eyes on my sleeve, and the bus stops with a loud, slow squeal and the robotic voice calls out, "Ocean View Drive."

We leave the bus, and Rachel leads the way through the dim light to the beach. We go to this cliff with about a million tiny stairs going down it. Even from the top, we can hear people walking up and down the steps. Farther on, there's the faint sound of laughter and drums.

At the bottom of the steps, the beach widens and there's a strong smell of smoke, from the bonfires and the pot. There are bunches of naked people lounging around the fires, and vendors selling trinkets and food right near the steps. Rachel holds out a hand.

"Okay, give me a tenner so we can get some vodka watermelon."

I reach into my pocket and pull out a ten. I haven't really had anything to drink before except a few sips of beer, but now seems like as good a time as any to learn how to drink. Even if it is in watermelon.

Rachel balances a large plate of sliced watermelon. We go and sit on some driftwood and suck the fiery-tasting melon. I sink the toes of my runners into the sand.

I divided $187 between my shoes, bra and underwear. I put the bills in plastic ziplock bags I took from Darla's kitchen. It seems like a lot of money, but it's not going to last long. I'll give myself twenty bucks to spend tonight, and then that's it. I gotta think of a plan.

"Hey." Rachel pokes me in the ribs. "Check it out."

There's a flaming circle moving toward us. A guy is in the middle of the flames, walking slow and steady, tossing fire with an easy grace. All casual, like he could have been whistling. He walks toward us, tossing the flaming sticks higher and higher, so that they look like long streaks of light.

He looks about eighteen, with a ballcap pulled low and a couple of tattoos on his bare shoulders. His arms flex every time he tosses up a burning torch, and there's a line of sweat trickling down his face. I can hear the *whoosh, whoosh* of the fire as it careens into the sky and back again. People gather around us. He juggles both sticks into one hand, pulls off his ballcap and throws it to the ground, close to our feet.

He starts juggling again, turning to face the crowd as he winks at Rachel and me. Rachel tries the through-the-eyelashes sexy stare. I concentrate on not reaching into my bra to dump a bagful of money into the empty hat.

"Welcome to the best traveling fire-breathing beach show in the world! My name is Tate, and I'll be your fire breather for tonight. If you're coming to watch me, you have my personal guarantee that I will not accidentally light any more than two of you on fire."

There's a small ripple of laughter in the crowd. A couple of cigarette ends glow brightly as people take a drag or light up and walk away.

"With this in mind," he continues, "I'd like to ask for a volunteer to help me with tonight's routine."

A few hands wave in the air, but he points at me. My heart skips a beat as I look up stupidly to see if my hand was in the air. It was not.

"How about you? Come on up here, cutie."

Rachel grabs my hand. "She's shy. But I'll help."

"I'll help." I shake Rachel off and walk over to the fire guy, who is now spinning the torches in an arc above his head, dangerously close to his dark brush cut. It looks like one solid arc of light, the fire chasing its own tail.

He flips the torches up and catches them in one clean movement.

"Are you afraid of fire, sweetie?"

I shake my head no, and he hands me two torches. "Good stuff. Hang on to these, will you?"

I hold the torches away from my body. Already I can feel the heat coming in waves near my face. He juggles the other two torches lightly, a quick back and forth between his hands.

"Now listen, I'm going to have you toss me a torch as I juggle these two. Toss too low, and you'll light my balls on fire. Toss too high, and my hair's going up. Actually, just to be safe, if you have to throw badly, throw badly *up high*."

The audience is loosening up now, giving him a few laughs. I know it's just for show, but part of me likes the way he half grins at me, like we're the only ones in on the real joke. I'm not nervous either. I'm a really good juggler, and I've won a couple of provincial rhythmic gymnastics events. Mom got it in her head that I was missing out by our moving so much, so she always put me in the same thing—gymnastics. Really, though, I think the first time she just needed to send me to camp for two months so she could get her head on straight. But I did like rhythmic gymnastics. I liked the certainty of gravity. I liked how whatever went spinning up into the sky would land solidly back in the palm of your hand.

"Okay, darling, when I say now, you throw that flame over here."

He's juggling the two torches over and under one leg. Even from close up, it looks like the orange flames are licking the hem of his shorts.

"Now!" He throws both torches up high, and I toss him another. He catches it lightly, and the audience claps as he incorporates it into a smooth juggle. Tate rewards me with another wink.

I can't help but show off a bit. I toss the remaining torch up, like the clubs in gymnastics. It's really the same thing. Only on fire.

It twirls and arcs in the night sky like a crazy star. The balance is good. I give a little spin and catch it behind my back.

The crowd *ooohs*, and I see him falter, almost miss a beat on the last torch, as he watches me. My skin burns with his gaze.

Chapter Five

"Looks like the lovely lady is trying to steal my show!" Tate recovers quickly and flashes me a grin as he juggles his torches. "Let's see what she's done to my heart." He brings up the three batons and angles them toward the sky, then leans in and blows on the flames until they leap up, a supernova of fire. Everyone *ooohs*, and I hear myself doing it too.

"I'd like to remind everyone that it costs ten bucks to go to a movie and you won't find anything real at the movies. Every show I do is dangerous, but I do it all for you, so if you like what you see, my hat is right there." He juggles the fire in a crazy arc, spinning it high into the air. "And now, folks, for a little piece I like to call You Are What You Eat."

With one hand still flipping the other batons, Tate easily catches the third and brings it to his mouth. The flaming torch flares orange and disappears into his mouth as he closes his lips around it. He pulls the extinguished end out and smiles at me and then quickly puts out the other two torches. The beach is suddenly dark, but the hazy white outline of the last flame burns into my eyes.

He picks up his hat and starts casually walking around the crowd. People throw in quarters and a few toonies. I yank a ten-dollar bill out of my pocket and walk up to him. I try to put it into the hat, but he grabs my hand lightly.

"Hey, beautiful, assistants don't have to pay."

I'm glad it's dark, because I can feel the red creeping up all over my face. I want to be smart and witty. I want to have the perfect thing to say. I want to tell him how it made me feel to see that rush of fire dance from his mouth.

"I want to pay. It was great, it was really…great."

"Tell you what." He throws his torches into a canvas bag and zips it up. "Let's leave this place and go out for drinks, and I'll call it even."

Out of the corner of my eye, I see Rachel shaking sand out of her shoes. I can't leave her and go with some guy I just met. I have this crazy urge to put my hand on his bare chest, to feel the ripple of muscle that runs there. He thinks I'm old enough to go for a drink. I could be anyone at all to him.

"I can't tonight." I could be the kind of girl to make him wait. "I have plans. But give me your number and I'll call you."

We don't have any paper, so he scribbles his number on my hand with a Sharpie. His handwriting is large and loopy, and his number tingles on my palm. He hangs on to my hand for a second longer and grins. "Anytime you need a light, give me a call."

I laugh. "Does that line ever work?"

"We'll see. Call me anyway."

He shoulders his bag and walks away, pants hung loose around his hips, his bare back starting to blend into the night.

"Holy shit, you got his number?" Rachel grabs my wrist and twists it around so that she can see the writing on my hand. "What is he, like, twenty? You have all the luck."

The next day, I head out to find a pay phone. I have to walk to the park to get to the only phone booth I've seen in ages. It's decrepit, and the booth smells like piss.

I take a breath as I slide the quarters into the slot and dial his number. The line clicks open on the second ring.

"Hello?"

"Hey, Tate, it's Ally calling." There's silence, and I add lamely, "From the show last night."

"Ally who isn't afraid of fire. I'm glad you called."

"Why is that?"

"Because I was thinking of you. I'm at the park on Twenty-Second Street, with some friends. Want to come and hang out?"

When I get to the park, I want to hide behind a tree and just watch him. He's surrounded by a few girls, and I can see the juggling pins flashing in all directions as he keeps up his chatter. The girls titter around him.

Screw it. What do I have to lose? I saunter up to the group, trying my best to look like a twenty-year-old who doesn't care about walking up to a group of strangers.

"Hey, fire girl! Catch." One of the girls moves to see who he's talking to. Tate tosses two pins my way, one after another. I catch them as I walk and toss them back, timing my rhythm to his.

He juggles the two pins back into his formation and grins at me.

"Ally here has a bit of circus freak in her, don't you?"

I shrug. "A bit. I'm good with juggling."

"And fire?"

The girls glare at me. The tall brunette rolls her eyes at her friend.

"Sure."

Tate catches the pins out of the air and smiles. He looks directly at me, and I feel wobbly. I felt better when I had something to do with my hands. Some reason to be talking to this guy, like the girls around him don't even exist.

The brunette gives a sniff and picks up her bag. "Tate, I gotta go. My shift's starting."

"Sure. See you later." She leaves, her friends trailing along.

Tate reaches into his open bag and brings out four more pins.

"Wanna play?"

Chapter Six

Tate tosses the pins at me so quickly that I can't do anything but concentrate on the rhythm of his juggling. We've got eight pins going now, and I can feel a small trickle of sweat running down the small of my back. I'd like to look as calm as he does. I seriously doubt I can flirt and juggle at the same time.

"You're pretty smooth with the pins. Have you ever done poi?"

"I don't think so." I can't tell if he's talking about juggling or drugs.

"It's awesome. I wish it were dark—I could show you fire poi. But you'll get the idea with this."

Tate reaches into his bag and pulls out a string with fluorescent round weights on either end. He tosses it into the air and then catches it deftly in the middle, spinning it until it looks like a single circle around him.

"I think I'm going to try some fire poi by the end of the festival season. I love the patterns that you can make when you're working with fire." He spins it and starts throwing it from hand to hand. "Want to try? You in those shorty shorts—I'll bet you'd dazzle everyone. You could call it *balls on fire*."

I lean forward and hit him in the chest. His skin is warm and soft. "You're awful. But yeah, I'll try."

He hands the poi to me and I toss it up, watching the way it heaves in the air and falls before I catch it in the center. The rope is smooth and comfortable in my palm. Rope was never my forte in rhythmic gymnastics, but the weights on either end make this seem more like clubs.

I toss it a few times, getting the feel of it, and then think, *Why not show him a little more of what I can do*? It hits me suddenly that gymnastics isn't as dorky when you're not in a sparkly outfit.

I toss the poi high up, do a front flip and land in the splits, one arm stuck out to catch the poi. It lands a foot away with an embarrassing thump. Of course.

"Holy shit!"

I don't want to look up at Tate. I'd like to gather what's left of my dignity and walk away and never see him again. But it's very hard to get up gracefully from the splits. I look up. Tate is holding the poi, and his forehead is creased.

"We should do an act together. If you can do that with it on fire, we would clean up!"

"I'm sure I could. Heck, I might even be able to catch it next time." Even as I say it, I can picture my hair on fire, acrid smoke rising from my bald and burnt scalp. Then he smiles, and I figure what the hell—I'm already on fire.

After an hour and a half of demonstrating my most back-bending moves, I feel gross and sticky.

Tate tosses the poi in his bag. "I'm hot. Let's go to the kiddie pool."

"Are we allowed?"

He throws his head back and laughs. His teeth are even and white. "It's a public park. And besides, who cares?"

The kiddie pool is at the end of the park. It's so shallow that not even a poorly supervised toddler could drown in it. Tate leans down and rolls up his jeans. I walk right into the pool. The water is beautifully cool. It's only up to my ankles, but it feels like my body temperature has dropped about five degrees.

Suddenly there's a cold dump of water over my head, and I yelp and turn around to find Tate standing just behind me, ready with another handful of water. I sprint for the other side of the pool, trying my best to skirt the google-eyed babies sitting all over the place. Tate catches the back of my T-shirt and pours the water down my neck. My feet get tangled up with his, and we splash down into the water, laughing. Tate leans down and kisses me softly. A flush of heat runs all through my body.

A park employee leans down and taps Tate on the shoulder. "Hey, love-birds, this is a pool for babies, not for making 'em. Get out."

Tate scrambles to his feet and offers his arm to help me up too. We're both dripping and grinning like idiots.

I step out of the pool and Tate follows, saying "Sorry" with a backward glance at the closest mother and then, "Nice baby."

"I'm soaked." Tate squeezes out his T-shirt. "I live around here. Why don't we go dry out at my apartment? It's not far."

I know I shouldn't. But I'm walking beside him, heart thumping, and he slips his hand in mine like it's the most natural thing in the world. Like I belong to him.

His apartment is a few floors up, a small bachelor with a boy-sized mess.

Clothes are strewn on the floor, and there are piles of dishes in the sink. I close the door. Tate presses me up against it, leaning his hard body into mine. His hands are on my waist, and it feels like he could lift me right up if he wanted to. He kisses me again, running his hands up my sides, lifting my shirt as he goes.

I feel light-headed, hot and cold at the same time. My wet T-shirt slides over my head, and some part of me that is still able to speak says, "No."

Tate stops short, his hand arrested on its path to my bra clasp. "No?"

I take a breath and try to slow my rushing blood. This is going too quick.

"Just…I just need a second. I mean, this is going a little fast for me."

Tate takes a step back and a long breath, with his eyes closed. Then he opens them up again and smiles at me. "Absolutely. I'm going to get a dry shirt. Do you want one?"

Chapter Seven

I have to remember to tuck my tank top into my shorts so that the stray material doesn't catch fire. It's these small things that have me nervous. Normally, if I screw up a routine, I end up with a few points docked, not third-degree burns.

My bedroom door opens. Rachel squeezes in and shuts the door behind her.

"I can't believe you're actually going to do this. Five bucks says you light yourself on fire."

"Make it ten. Let's get going."

When we get to the beach, Tate isn't there yet. I unpack the supplies he gave me and lay them out in a neat line. I can see people watching me, and I want to make it seem like I know what I'm doing. Rachel hasn't shut up since we left the house.

"So, what's your stage name, Ally? You should totally go for something Asian—people love that. Like maybe the Chinese Dragon. Or Mei-Mei the Fire Queen."

I laugh. "Oh screw off. What are you? The White Wraith?"

Rachel pouts and looks at her skin. "I'm getting tan." Then she brightens. "There's your man. I'm looking forward to the ten bucks."

Tate is coming, hat pulled down low over his eyes. Even from here I can see the grin playing at the edge of his lips. That's part of what I love about him, the way he always looks delighted and amused when he sees me. A flush of heat runs down my body. I wish the show were over so we could get to the secluded logs on the far side of the beach that we've claimed for the last two weeks.

The routine is simple—I could have done it when I was ten—but it depends on me not getting distracted when Tate throws me a club or winks at me or juggles with his shirt off. Tate puts an arm around me and leans down to kiss me deeply. He takes his time. When he finally lifts his head, he smiles at me.

"Ready?"

"You bet."

Tate lights up three torches and hands them to me, then lights another three. By now the weight of the torches is familiar, but I'm still getting used to the whoosh of heat that comes in waves over my face and hands.

"Ladies and gentleman, dressed and naked, come and behold the best fire show on the beach."

Tate starts to juggle his three flaming torches and I do the same, finding comfort in the regular rhythm of the simple juggle. The clubs slap into my hands easily, and I feel myself start to loosen up.

Tate winks at me. On cue, we each toss a club to the other and watch the arc of fire in the dark blue sky as the torches pass close enough that it seems like they're part of the same flame. There's a rustle as people draw nearer, and I see one woman leaning back, hand over her heart.

The flames make their own sound, too, a cross between that of wind and suction.

I toss two clubs to Tate, and he juggles all five with ease. I have the last club, and this is where we're supposed to awe the crowd. I give it two long spins in the air, watch the wind massage the flames slightly to the right and then give it a hard toss forward and straight ahead. The club spins crazily in the air. I picture my body as flame as I spring into a backflip, land into the splits and then wait for the torch to land neatly in my hand. The moment it hits, there's wild applause. I spring up, lean all the way back and catch the other torch that Tate tosses to me from his juggling. Bent back, I spin the torches in opposite directions, right myself, and then spin around until it seems like I'm surrounded by a circle of fire.

There is a drawn-out *oooh* from the crowd. Tate is blowing fire above me, and even though he's pretty far away, the heat ricochets off the top of my head. I'm so glad it's a windless night. He tosses all the clubs back to me save one, which he swallows. One by one, I toss him another club out of my juggling formation until the last one disappears in his mouth.

There's a pause after the beach is suddenly plunged into darkness, and then the applause begins. Tate barely has to do a speech before the hat starts getting filled with folding money. The crowd starts to get up and go, but there's a small gathering around me, talking excitedly. I can just see Tate through the crowd. He is stuffing money from the hat into his pocket when he sees me and flashes the thumbs-up. I'm breathing hard. All of a sudden, I'm aware of my heart going at double speed. I had forgotten the rush of performing, how it takes you away from yourself. For those five minutes it was nothing but fire and my body—a controlled burn.

Tate is working his way through the crowd. He puts his hand on my back, leans down to kiss me. His lips are warm. He tastes like paraffin and s'mores.

"Oh my god, you were great! You would kill at the festivals. I hate that I have to leave in a week. I'll miss you like crazy." He brushes my hair away from my face, and I make the decision then and there.

"You might be surprised."

Chapter Eight

"Ally, you're crazy. He might not even want you along." Rachel is sitting on my bed, pulling the loose thread on the blanket into one ginormous tangled mess.

I sigh. We've been through this a couple of times. "Pass me that T-shirt." Rachel hands it over, and I stuff it into the duffel bag. "I think I know him pretty well. We've spent the last month together,

Sarah Yi-Mei Tsiang

like every single minute. Besides, he practically invited me."

"Practically is pretty far from actually."

"Look. You and me, we have no future here. Do you know what they give you when you're eighteen? A kick out the door and a *have a nice life.* I'm just changing my temporary situation. At least I can make some money over the summer and maybe figure out how I'm going to live the rest of my life with no parents, no education, no friends and no support." I finish packing the duffel bag. I try not to think about how all my things don't even fill the stupid bag.

Lately, I've been trying not to think about a lot of stuff. Like the fact that Tate probably isn't coming back after the festivals but going to some college out east. Or that I probably won't be able to afford to go to university. Or that my mom is in a cardboard box at the bottom of my luggage.

I lift the bag to my shoulder and gesture to the door.

"You said you'd do me this favor. Try to make sure that Darla doesn't know I'm gone for as long as possible. I don't want to have to worry about cops looking for me before I can even get the bus ticket."

Rachel gets up and gives me a hug. "Okay. I'll do it. Don't get raped and don't get stabbed, and come back if you're piss poor and on your ass."

"Touching. I will."

The bus depot is huge and smells like a cross between a urinal and a tailpipe. I wait in line at the ticket counter and try to think of how best to surprise Tate. I know we can make more money together than we could separately, and I have enough for my bus ticket, so cash shouldn't be an issue. I'm hoping he's the kind of guy to take surprises in stride. Maybe I'll bring it up after a few kisses so he gets the idea that it might be nice to be out on the road together for a month.

I take a seat in one of the red plastic chairs and fiddle with my ticket. I know the name of the first town he's going to for a festival, but none after that. People drift in and out of the waiting room, chewing on hot dogs, dragging suitcases, giving one another prolonged, teary hugs.

I watch an old man as he methodically takes items out of his fanny pack and places them on the bench beside him. First a little bottle of pills, then a change purse and, lastly, a tube of Preparation H.

I look away from the Preparation H and there's Tate, standing over me.

"Ally! What are you doing here?"

"Surprise!" I make a little ta-da gesture with my hands and immediately regret it.

"Surprise what?" He makes it sound like the response to a bad knock-knock joke. I feel my palms start to sweat.

"Well, I thought I'd come with you. You said I'd kill in the festivals. We'll make a lot of cash together."

Tate sits down beside me and runs his hands through his hair. He rests his head on one hand and looks at me sideways.

"Ally, what the hell? I like you and everything, but I don't think this is what you think it is."

I can barely get out my words. "Oh? What is it?"

"It was...nicc. It was a nice month with you, but we're not exclusive or anything."

There's a burst of static, and then a female voice comes over the intercom. "Now boarding, bus eleven to Newport, Grenville, Beamsville."

Tate gets up. "I'm sorry it had to end this way."

"Yeah." I grip my ticket. What is there to go back to? I start to head to the line, and Tate grabs my elbow.

"What are you doing? I just said I'm going alone."

I feel a sudden rush of hot anger. "You're not my only option, asshole. Go wherever you're going. I have other plans."

We stand next to each other in the lineup, trying to avoid eye contact. I take a seat midway down the bus and stare out the window. Tate moves to the back. The doors of the bus close with a mechanical sigh, and we're pitched forward as the bus leaves the depot. I lean my head against the metal frame of the window and feel the hum of the road run through me. Forget crows. Buses are harbingers of doom.

How many buses have I been on in my lifetime? How many places did Mom and I move to? I feel a twist in my stomach. I'm running away from my life too. I guess the apple doesn't fall far from the tree. This time, though, I'm running alone.

The fields rush by in a green blur. Every town looks the same from a bus window. Same convenience stores, same run-down houses, same Walmarts with their one token windmill spinning hopelessly in the vast parking lot.

"Newport. This stop is Newport. Fifteen minutes."

I get up and clutch my duffel bag. I walk away from Tate without looking back. The bus driver has opened up the compartment under the bus, and a few people are grabbing their suitcases.

Tate's red bag is there. The one with all of his clubs and fire-breathing supplies.

I walk over, nod to the bus driver and take the bag.

I put Tate's bag over my shoulder and start walking down the road that looks like it leads into town. I can hear the bus behind me, and I step off the road to make way. In the last window, Tate glances out, sees me with his bag and bangs his fist on the pane of glass.

I lift my hand and watch him speed out of my life.

Chapter Nine

The town is up ahead, and right now I would trade everything I have for some air-conditioning and a hamburger. And a tall Coke in an icy glass, the kind that makes your hand all wet and cool when you pick it up.

Main Street boasts a takeout KFC place, a convenience store and more than a few shuttered businesses. At the end of the street is a sign for Debbie's Diner. I head there, hoping it'll be as cheap as it looks. I don't need to look into my bag to know that I have only $120 left for the rest of the summer.

The door of the diner opens with a welcome blast of air-conditioning. With a little shiver, I feel the sweat on my arms drying up. It's heaven. There's only one customer in the place, an old man in a plaid shirt, drinking coffee at the counter. I sit down at a booth with a long plastic bench and order a hamburger, fries and Coke. Halfway through it, my situation hits home. I thought I'd be spending the summer with Tate and making cash at the festivals. Tate said you can make a couple thousand dollars if you have a really good run. At the very least, I thought I'd have someone to be with. Now I'm alone with no idea of what to do next. Thank God I have Tate's stuff, or else I wouldn't even be able to busk. I'll need to find a place this afternoon to set up. Maybe I can make some money and figure out where to go next.

When the bill comes, I count out the money and leave a meager tip. Another $10 down the drain. I grab my stuff and head out the door before the waitress can give me a dirty look.

I find a park close to the downtown. It's not huge, but it has a statue of some old guy and a little play structure. There are a couple of moms gossiping on the park bench. I figure this is as good a place as any. I unzip Tate's bag and take out the clubs. I know I should do a fancy introduction like Tate does, but I can't bring myself to talk to the bored-looking moms. Hopefully, the spectacle will draw them.

I don't want to accidentally set any toddlers on fire, so I take the practice clubs. Tate attached ribbons to the ends to give me an idea of how the fire extended the reach of the club. I start with a simple three-club juggle, and the kids begin to wander over. I add another two clubs and start practicing my fancier moves, the under-the-leg-trick, the clubs-way-up-high. The kids clap, and the moms start to wander over as well. I have a good little audience by the time I add in some basic gymnastics, like backflips and one-handed cartwheels.

I finish with a flourish, and everyone applauds. I clear my throat and try to use Tate's pitch for money. "So, um, if you've enjoyed the show, remember that a movie is ten dollars…"

I trail off as I realize that I don't have anything to collect the money in. A few of the moms are already wandering off after their kids. One little girl approaches me shyly and hands me a dollar. Then she runs back and buries her face in her mom's skirt.

I pocket it and wave to the moms, trying hard not to be bitter about their cheapness. A dollar for a full performance of backbreaking work. I'm sure they're all headed back to their air-conditioned houses and full pantries.

My back is coated with sweat, and I'm pretty sure I stink. I need to perform tonight with fire. That's where the real money is.

The fleabag motel on the edge of town is $65 a night, but it feels worth it as soon as I step into the tiny bath. Warm water rushes over me, and I lie there watching the shampoo bubbles die. When I was a kid, I used to love taking baths, but we mostly had shower stalls. I think I liked the tubs best because Mom would stay with me and hang her arms over the edge. She would take a wash-cloth and scrub my back and hum under her breath. I liked the echo of her voice, and the small dripping sounds.

I grab the corner of the towel and scrub the tears off my face. I have to make back the motel money by the end of the night.

The park is empty, and while Newport doesn't exactly have a swinging night-life, there are a few more people around now, eating on patios and taking dinner-time strolls.

I set up in front of one of the abandoned stores. It doesn't have an awning, so I don't have to worry about setting the store on fire. I will have to be extra careful with the wind, though, or I'll get a face full of flames when it blows my way. My supplies are lined up in front of me, and I have Tate's bag open and ready to receive cash. I sprinkle in a few dollars to prime the pump.

"Ladies and gentleman"—I already sound like a loser—"prepare yourself for the greatest fire show in all of Newport."

I light the clubs and start juggling. A small crowd starts to gather, and I can hear their whispered *ooohs* and *aahs* as I toss the clubs higher and higher. A few people press closer.

"Back up, please." I can feel sweat beading around my forehead. "I really don't want to light any of you on fire."

A couple of people shuffle back a half-step. I try to take a step backward, but I hit the wall behind me. One older lady gets jostled from behind, and she steps too close to me. A few people call *Watch it!* and I step forward quickly to intercept the flaming club that is bearing down on her, but it's halfway through its spin and my wrist hits the flames instead.

"Ow! Shit!" The clubs clatter to the ground.

A murmur runs through the crowd, and some people back up, but most of them walk away. I relight the torches, hoping people won't notice that my hands are shaking. My wrist is killing me. I'm doing a basic juggle for the few people who have stayed when I see the fire truck pull up to the curb.

I blow out the clubs and clamp a hand over my throbbing wrist. The skin is red and starting to blister. I fold up my things as the firefighters walk up.

"Miss, hang on. We need to talk to you."

The last few audience members walk away, glancing over their shoulders at me.

The older firefighter frowns at me. "What were you doing here?"

"Just busking." I can feel my face getting red.

"You can't just juggle fire out in the open. Do you have a permit?"

"I'm sorry. It was stupid—I won't do it again." I'm praying that they won't call the cops.

"No, you won't." As if he's reading my mind, he adds, "I could call the cops, you know. Have you charged with endangerment of life."

"Please." I hold up my hands in supplication. "No one was hurt."

He grabs my elbow gently. "Looks like you were." He turns my wrist over and sighs. "It's not bad. Come to the truck and I'll patch you up. Do your parents know you're doing this?"

I nod my head. "But I normally do it on a beach."

After he bandages my wrist, he hands me a ticket. "I'm going to go easy on you. It's a ticket for open-air burning. I figure your wrist was enough of a warning tonight. You can pay the hundred and fifty dollars at city hall tomorrow. " He pauses and then gives me a fatherly pat on the back. "No more playing with fire now, you hear?"

Chapter Ten

The motel checkout is 11:00 AM, and I'm waiting out the clock. I don't want to leave this small room that has a shower and a TV and air-conditioning. Besides, I'm waiting for the manager to come and check out the room and give me back my cash damage deposit. I wish I had a credit card.

The manager shows up at ten thirty. He's lean and pasty-looking, with greasy hair. The kind of guy who talks directly to your breasts.

I open the door and gesture behind me. "Everything's good. I even made the bed."

He comes in and starts poking around. He points to a dent in the bed frame that's probably been there since 1959. "This bed was in mint condition. Your deposit is going to have to cover the cost of repairs."

"That's bullshit! This shitty room is no more shitty than it was when I took it."

He leans against the cheap bed. "I'm keeping the deposit. I'll call the cops for vandalism if you like."

He's got me. Worse, he's got my $40 deposit on top of the room fee. I grab my bags and walk out to the parking lot. It's so hot, it feels like the asphalt is melting under my thin sandals. I have the ticket from last night buried in my bag. With the ticket, I am now officially in debt to the city. I don't want to risk seeing Tate, but I'm going to have to hit the festival. It's the only way I can dig myself out of this hole.

My stomach is grumbling. I can't afford a bus ticket, so I get a half dozen donuts and a bottle of water with my last few bucks. I'm so hungry, I eat three donuts at the shop, then wrap up the rest and put them in my bag. I figure the sugar will keep me going for at least a little while.

I walk just past the bus stop on the highway. I've never hitched before, but it seems pretty simple. Stick out your leg, stick out your thumb and hope you don't get a pervert.

A bunch of cars zoom by without slowing down. I pick up my bags and start walking. The road shimmers ahead of me, heat dancing like flames. I have to keep stopping and pulling out my water bottle. At this pace, I'll get there by next year. I wish I could dump the water over my head and wash away some of the sweat, but who knows when I'll be able to refill the bottle?

A transport truck honks long and loud, and I scramble to the far side of the shoulder. He pulls over ahead of me, and his brakes give a metallic screech. I run to the side of the truck and open the door of the cab.

"Where you headed, darlin'?"

"Beamsville."

"Hop in, then."

We travel in silence for a few minutes, me twisting my hands in my lap.

"So, uh, how long have you been driving?" I finally say.

He laughs. "A long time. Longer than you've been hitching."

"How would you know how long I've been hitching?"

"You're young. What, a runaway?
Fight with Mom and Dad?"

I hug Tate's bag of supplies to my
chest. "I'm a busker. I'm headed over to
Beamsville for the festival there."

He nods wisely. "I gotcha. Going to
join the circus. Well, none of my busi-
ness. But I'll bet that there's someone
missing you."

"I hope you're not a betting man,
then."

He gives me a sidelong look. "Just
a tip, honey. If you're alone and you're
traveling, you'd better tell strange men
that there's someone waiting for you at
the other end."

Beamsville is much bigger than
Newport, and the downtown ends at
a large lake. There are fancy restau-
rants all over town, especially on the
main street, where patios extend onto

the large sidewalk and throw a few cooling shadows from their oversized umbrellas. The festival starts tomorrow. I want to wait and see where the buskers are setting up before I try to sneak my own act in.

I've finished the last of my donuts, and I'm already starting to get hungry again. I head to one of the parks to practice with the clubs. I find an open space and start juggling, but it's hard to concentrate with all the hot-dog vendors around. My stomach starts rumbling every time one of the vendors puts another dog on the grill. The sun beats down on the top of my head, and when I go to pick up one of the dropped clubs, I feel weak and dizzy. I stumble to my knees and sit in the grass for a minute before I can make my way over to the shade of a nearby tree.

A mom walks over and places a Styrofoam takeout container in the garbage can beside me. I wait until she leaves, then open it up. I see most of a hot dog and some ketchup-soaked fries. It still looks good—there are only two small bites out of the hot dog. I sit back down on the grass and take a bite out of the intact end of the hot dog. It's still warm.

I finish the lunch and rummage through my bag for the bottle of water. It's empty. My shoulders are aching from hauling my luggage around, but I grab the bags again and head out in search of a public washroom.

The library is a couple of blocks away from the downtown core, but it's huge and beautiful. I fill up my water bottle and gulp from the water fountain, letting the cool liquid run down my chin. I wander around a bit and pick up a book at random, a biography of Winston Churchill. There are plush armchairs all around, and I'm just settling in for a nap when a voice comes over the intercom announcing that it's closing time.

I leave the book and slink into the bathroom. I close the stall door and squat on the seat so that no one can see my feet. Hopefully, they'll close up the library and I can ride the night out on a couch.

The noises from the library die down, but then the bathroom door squeaks open. I can hear the security guard opening each stall in turn. The guard comes to my stall and knocks on the door. I lose my nerve.

"Just a minute." I flush, and then I open the door.

"Library's closed, miss."

I go back to the park. The benches are all empty, so I choose one close to the water and curl up. The first star glimmers in the distance. I read once that some of the stars we see exploded thousands of years ago. It's just that the light takes so long to get here.

I want to stay awake. Part of me thinks that this star is already dead and I'm the only one who can keep it alive by watching the last of its glimmer. But it disappears as my eyelids pull shut.

Chapter Eleven

The cops are putting up roadblocks
along the main street for the festival.
They don't even glance my way, but
they still make me nervous. Officially,
I'm a runaway, and I'll bet my picture
is up there somewhere in the cop
shop. Once the festival is in full gear,
I'm sure I can just slip into a spot and
start performing. If anyone realizes I'm

not on the list, I'll be gone by the time they think to ask me for a permit.

The buskers are supposed to perform on the main road, and the audience stands on the sidewalk. I took a performance schedule from the library, and I figure I can slip into the spaces where there's supposed to be a ten-minute break between half-hour acts.

The first break is between a whip artist and a strong-woman act. The whip artist arrives a little early to set up. He's a pudgy old white guy with a funny little mustache. As soon as people see him start to set up, a crowd gathers.

He straps on a portable mic and his voice booms across the street.

"Welcome to the whip show, an amazing display of strength, danger and, of course"—he pauses here and runs his hands down his beer belly—"raw sexuality." The audience laughs, and he grins with them as he reaches into his bag to take out a huge whip. He flashes it in the air. The whip cracks with a loud bang.

The show is amazing. He whips an apple off a guy's head, plays a song using his whip and some half-filled beer bottles and keeps up a hilarious patter all the way through. The audience is in stitches. At the end of his act he gives the standard speech asking for money. A good chunk of the crowd just walks away, but a lot of people reach into their purses and pockets and pull out a few bucks. It would be more than enough for a motel, some food and maybe even a bus ticket.

He packs up his bag and steps off the street. I take a deep breath and look around. No one seems to be monitoring the space, and there's still a sizable chunk of the crowd here, milling around and talking.

I step onto the street and say in my loudest voice, "Welcome, ladies and gents, to the best fire show in all the world."

A bunch of people turn around, and I think of the old lady who almost caught fire.

"I know you'd all like to see the fire up close, but I'll need you to make a large circle around me so that no one ends up too horrifically burned. Except hecklers, of course."

The crowd laughs as they settle in, and the kids sit cross-legged on the edge of the sidewalk. Because the street is closed off, people seem to settle naturally on the sidewalk instead of edging into the street.

I take out Tate's Kevlar torches and dip them into the lamp oil. They light up with a burst of flame as the excess oil burns off. I flip the torches into a juggle and look around.

"Who wants to see a forward-backward juggle?" There's a smattering of clapping and cheering, so I walk back and forth while juggling, and the crowd groans.

"I'm just kidding. Here it is." I have the three torches in the air. I catch each one and give them an extra spin so that the flame shoots toward me and completes a full turn before landing back in my hand. The heat is killer, but it's still a pretty safe trick on a windless day like today.

"Let's get this crowd going! If you all cheer loud enough, I'll backflip while throwing my torches. If you cheer even louder, I'll try to catch the torches instead of just whipping them into the crowd like I normally do."

I throw the torches higher and higher, and as the crowd seems to hold its breath, I shout out, "Ready? Now let's hear you!"

I'm half braced for complete silence, so it's a relief when the crowd erupts. I hold two torches, give the last an extra-high toss, do a quick backflip and land with plenty of time to catch the third torch. The applause is fast and hard, and it feels like my heartbeat, out of control and wild.

Already I can picture the money I'm going to get. Two women push through the crowd in glitzy outfits, and I realize that I've completely lost track of time. They're obviously the next act, the pair of strong women. It's hard to look at your watch when you're supposed to be looking at your torches. The two women are glaring at me, but I haven't collected my money. They look fighting mad. I've been in a few fights in my life, but never with oiled-up muscle women in spangled bodysuits.

Chapter Twelve

The women push through the crowd, and I know that my chance to collect money has just gone up in smoke.

The taller of the two, a brunette, walks with a swagger right up to me. I catch my torches and hold them in one hand. She leans over and blows them out with one breath, then turns to the audience, flipping on her head mic.

"Let's hear it for our amateur opening act, Fire Girl!" The other woman walks up to me and raises my other hand in mock victory, like a boxer.

The tall one continues, "We're your scheduled professional act, Strong Women Extraordinaire! I'm Lorna and this is Sandy." As she says this, the shorter, wiry blond, Sandy, is still holding my arm in a viselike grip. She walks me to the edge of the crowd while waving and then covers her mic with her hand and whispers in my ear. "This is our spot. Get lost."

Sandy does a double front flip to the middle of the street, landing a few inches away from Lorna. Lorna bends into a full back arch. Sandy places her hands on Lorna's thighs and hoists herself up as if she were on a balancing beam. There's a hushed murmur from the crowd as she holds the position like an Olympic gymnast. They're both perfectly still, and then Sandy lifts her legs behind her with perfect precision so that she ends up in a handstand on Lorna.

Their act is breathtaking but silent. They make it look too easy, and some of the crowd starts to melt away. I can't believe their control. Not a muscle shakes as they lift and contort themselves into incredibly impossible positions. When they wrap up their act, they give a short speech about the money and then pass around the hat.

There are way fewer people putting in money for them than for the whip guy. Most of the families with kids got bored halfway through and left. I know most of those families would have given me money if I had had a chance to collect. Being funny pays. Some of the cash in the strong women's hat is rightfully mine. I wait until the crowd has dispersed and then walk up to them.

Strong women or not, I can't afford for them to walk away with my cut.

"Hey. I worked up the crowd for you. I didn't get a chance to collect. Half of that money should be mine."

Sandy, who is holding the hat, frowns. "Look, kid, this was our act, our spot and our money."

"My name is Ally, not *kid*. I worked hard for that money too, and I want my cut."

Lorna walks over and stands with her feet wide apart, her arms folded. She looks even bigger this way, like a brick wall. "Why are we even talking about this?"

I square my shoulders, painfully aware that I'm less than half her size. "Your take isn't half of what it should be. You lose most of your audience partway through." I give my torches a little juggle. "Count your take. If you put me in your act, I'll bet you get more than double what you made this afternoon."

Sandy puts a hand on Lorna's shoulder. "Look, you seem like a good kid, but we're professionals. I doubt very much that you could double our take."

"Give me a chance. One act. If I don't double your take, I won't get any of the cut."

I can tell Sandy is wavering. She looks up at Lorna with raised eyebrows.

Lorna sighs loudly. "Give us a minute."

They walk away, and Sandy does most of the talking. She's leaner than Lorna and reminds me of a bird—all quick movements and lots of energy. They walk back to me, and Lorna gestures to my torches. "Show us what you can do first, and we'll consider it. Fire amateurs are the worst." She says the last part pointedly.

The street is still pretty empty, so I have enough room to work. I prepare the torches and tell them to stand back a bit. I start with some light juggling just to warm up. I move quickly to my back-flip-and-catch routine and then to the splits-and-stand juggle. I can tell Lorna is grudgingly impressed.

A crowd is already starting to form, and I can't help but grin at Sandy and Lorna. Fire is flashy. I tell them to move the crowd back, and I take a breath. This is my one real chance to make an impression. If I want to get a real spot, I had better pull out all the stops.

Fire breathing makes me more nervous than the rest of the act. I've only done it twice with Tate, and he told me some horror stories about people getting nervous and sucking the flames into their faces instead of out front. The treetops aren't moving, and I can't even feel a whisper of wind against my face.

I take a swig of oil and hold up the torch. The trick is not to spit but to spray the oil in an even, steady arc. And not to swallow.

I squeeze my lips together and spray out the oil, watching my breath become flame. The crowd *ooohs* and everyone takes a step back, even though they're at a safe distance. The fire leaps out into the sky. It feels like I'm actually breathing flames, like everything inside of me is rushing out in a roaring explosion.

It takes a few seconds for the oil to run out, and the flame disappears in midair. The audience erupts into applause and whistles. I grab my bottle of water and rinse out my mouth. Some of the people come and hand me cash, and a couple drop coins into the bag at my feet.

Lorna extends her hand, and I shake it. It's hard not to marvel at the solid muscles that bulge from her shoulder to her forearm. "Looks like we're sharing a spot, Fire Girl."

Sandy punches me lightly on the arm. "All right, Ally. Let's meet up here in a hour and figure out how you can work with us without setting us on fire. Lorna and I are going to grab dinner."

Chapter Thirteen

I walk in the opposite direction as Sandy and Lorna so that it looks like I have someplace to go for dinner. My adrenaline is still pumping, but my hunger is catching up quickly. Restaurant patios are pushed out to the sidewalk, and the whole street smells like food. If I wait around a bit, I might be able to grab some food off a plate before the waiter comes by to collect the dirty dishes. I take a couple passes by some of the tables to see if anyone is close to finishing. There's a young couple playing footsies under the table, not giving much thought to their food. I pretend to bend down and fiddle with my shoelaces. He puts some money on the table and they leave, hand in hand.

I walk over quickly and grab a handful of fries and the rest of his roast beef sandwich. The money on the table is tempting, but Mom used to wait tables, and I hate to think of the waitress getting stuck with the bill.

I head over to the library to freshen up in the public bathroom. It's hard to get really clean with paper towels and hand soap. The paper towels disintegrate into little brown rolls along my skin. I splash some extra water on my face. The dripping figure in the mirror looks nothing like me. My skin is really dark, and there's a sunburn running across the top of my nose and cheekbones. The skin is already starting to peel. I run my wet fingers through my tangled black hair, but it just makes me look like even more of a hobo.

Sandy and Lorna are waiting for me at the park. They're easy to spot—they would stand out in just about any crowd. Lorna looks like one of those bodybuilders who can pop out individual muscles for the judges. She's got cropped brown hair and is evenly tanned too, but without the orangey spray-on tan that's so popular with bodybuilders. Sandy is stretching out on a park bench, and though she has muscles, they're long and lean like a dancer's.

Sandy spots me first and waves her hand. "Over here, Ally."

Lorna still looks a little guarded, but she offers me a small smile. "Our next performance is at 10:00 PM. If you want in on that one, we'd better find a way to make this act look like we've been doing it for more than an afternoon."

"I had a few ideas when I was watching your performance," I say. "Can you do that standing-on-each-other thing again?"

Lorna gets down on one knee and Sandy steps with both feet into Lorna's left hand. Lorna stands up slowly, holding Sandy with one hand. She lifts Sandy up above her head, her left arm steady as a rock.

Next comes my favorite part. Sandy bends over, puts both hands into Lorna's extended right hand and lifts herself slowly into a handstand in the air.

I circle them, watching for any twitches, any signs that they might wobble.

"How long can you guys hold that?"

Sandy twists her head to look at me, still perfectly straight over Lorna. "At least a full minute. Probably two."

I take out my torches and stand in front of Lorna. We're about the same height, nose to nose.

"I won't light the torches, but here's what I could do."

I extend my arms to juggle behind Lorna's back. The torches need to be really high to make this work. With Sandy and Lorna together, they're a little over ten feet tall. The trick is twofold—I need to throw the torches high enough to clear Sandy and with enough control to move the fire all the way around them.

The torches are going higher and higher. I want them over Sandy's feet for maximum effect.

"We'd be doing this on fire, so I want a good clearance."

Sandy grimaces. "So it's my toes potentially on fire, right?"

"Lorna's not going to drop you, and I'm not going to set you on fire."

All three of us are sweating like overweight wrestlers now. I move backward slowly, bringing the torches closer and closer to upside-down Sandy until they pass right over her and I'm juggling in front of them.

Sandy backflips off Lorna and wipes her forehead with her arm. I catch the torches in one hand.

"What do you think? We could call it the ring of fire."

Sandy grabs Lorna's hand. "You see? It's a sign."

I look at the two of them. "What sign?"

Sandy wiggles the ring finger of her left hand. "It's our wedding song, 'Ring of Fire.' Lorna's a huge Johnny Cash fan."

Lorna shrugs and gives me a small smile.

"I love Johnny too. I grew up listening to him."

Sandy laughs. "You're still growing up. How old are you, anyway?"

"Eighteen. I'm just making a bit of money for college."

Lorna exchanges a look with Sandy and then picks up one of my torches.

"All right, what else do we have?"

By nine in the evening, we've got a pretty good routine down. I want to save what fuel I have left, so we don't practice with live flames. I don't mention that I don't have any money to buy more fuel. Hopefully, our next show will change that.

Chapter Fourteen

Sandy rummages through her bag and pulls out a sparkly bodysuit. She holds it up in front of me.

"It might be a bit baggy, but at least you'll match us."

I don't want to hurt Sandy's feelings, but there's no way I'm wearing a sequined bodysuit. My life might be tragic, but it's not that tragic. Yet.

Lorna sees the look on my face, and I get the feeling she didn't want to wear those outfits either. "Ally is a different act, babe. Just let her wear what she normally does."

Sandy sighs and folds up the suit. "All right. But at the least, we need a name for you, Ally. You're not really a strong woman."

"Yeah." I consider the name they called me when I crashed their time slot. "I'm not partial to amateur fire girl."

Lorna grins. "Sorry about that."

I like their name, Strong Women Extraordinaire, because it's simple and it's what they are. I don't feel extraordinary. But in the best parts of my routine, I feel like something bigger than myself. I feel like everything combustible in me flares up and is made visible. Like everything I've wanted to say comes out as fire, and it burns, and it doesn't.

"How about Girl On Fire?"

Sandy nods her head. "As long as that's a figurative, not a literal, name."

The show tonight is on the beach. I check and recheck my torches and fuel. My oil supply is running really low, but I'm hoping it's enough to get me through the act tonight. If I don't double their money tonight, I'll be left without any scheduled spots, which means I'll never make enough money to get by. Lorna and Sandy made just under $300 for their last act. I'll have to make sure we get at least $600 tonight. I try not to think of the fact that I had never made that much money with Tate. I glance at Lorna, who is limbering up with some splits and arm stretches. I'm just as good as they are. But I need to be better at getting the money in the end.

Lorna finishes her warm-up and waves me over. "We're starting in five. I'll give you my head mic tonight to see what you can do with the crowd."

Already people are starting to wander over, brochures in hand. I take a deep breath. Why should I be afraid of the crowd? I'm the one with the flaming torches.

I light up and start juggling. "Welcome, ladies and gents, and especially people in fire-resistant clothing. I'm Girl On Fire, and these are my partners, Lorna and Sandy, otherwise known as Strong Women Extraordinaire."

Sandy flicks on the music, and a beat starts pumping.

"Who wants to see me throw a ring of fire around Lorna?" The crowd cheers politely, and Lorna gives them a wave and backflips to me, landing in a handstand. I do the ring of fire around her, tossing the torches at their regular height, and the crowd starts to become more interested.

The music helps too—it gives us a rhythm, and I make the torches land in my hand on the same beat as the bass. I bring the torches close to Lorna's feet, and the crowd draws forward a little.

"Don't worry. I'm not going to set the little piggies on fire," I say, and Lorna wiggles her toes obligingly.

The ring of fire passes over Lorna, and the crowd cheers.

"You think that's good? How about we double that trick?" Lorna bends down and offers her hand to Sandy, who climbs on. A little *oooh* runs through the crowd as Lorna lifts Sandy over her head. Then there's a large collective gasp as Sandy takes Lorna's other hand and lifts her slowly into a handstand. We do the second ring of fire, this time with the torches speeding into the air at over ten feet high. At night, it looks like a complete circle of flames. I can see that Lorna and Sandy are both sweating, holding on to one another. I'd like to lean in and assure them that

I really won't light them on fire. I wink at Lorna instead when I pull the ring of fire over Sandy, and Lorna just rolls her eyes, but she's also grinning with relief.

Sandy hops off and raises her arms, gymnast-style. "That was ring of fire, ladies and gents, and we're just getting started."

Lorna takes Sandy's hands as she bends backward into a perfect half plank, while Sandy, suspended on Lorna's thighs, extends her feet so that they become a living platform. I blow out two torches and keep a single lit one in my hand. I'm a little nervous about stepping on Lorna and Sandy, but their balance is truly perfect. I place one foot on Lorna and the other on Sandy so that I'm standing on the two of them.

"I'm going to throw this torch forward, do a front flip and, hopefully, land and catch that same torch." A few people are still coming by, so I point out a woman who has pushed her way through and nudged her kid to the front. "That's right, ma'am, a line of protective children is a great idea, just in case I don't make the catch."

I feel Lorna's stomach muscles flex and know that she's straining. Taking care not to press down on them while I leap off, I toss the torch high and forward and flip off quickly, landing neatly and with enough time to lean and catch the torch, which went off a little too far to the right. The wind is picking up now—it's enough to push the torches a little off center.

The crowd is really into it now, and it's perfectly timed. With this wind, I need to wrap the show up. I give Sandy our hand signal. I'm not willing to do the fire-breathing finale if it's going to blow back in my face.

I light all three torches again and take a deep breath. Some people say that you make your money based on how well you ask for it, not on how good your act is.

I flip the torches and walk around the perimeter of the crowd, trying to make eye contact with as many people as I can. "Okay, people, I'm about to do the most dangerous stunt of all. I hope you liked the show, and I hope you think that risking our lives to entertain you is worth something in folding money. Just remember that a movie costs ten bucks, and they don't light anyone on fire. Now, if I could ask everyone who wants to remain at their current temperature to take three steps back."

I line up with Lorna and Sandy and take a last look at the crowd before I light my torches. When I flick my lighter on, my hands start to shake. I recognize a face in the middle of the crowd. *Tate.* I nod to Lorna and Sandy and tighten my lips. I hope they won't notice how my torches are quivering. We leap into our alternate ending together—a triple backflip, with me handing one torch to Lorna and one to Sandy and all of us ending upright, each with a torch. The flames sizzle and flare as we land, and the crowd cheers before pressing forward and shoving dollars into Sandy's canvas bag. Tate claps, his eyes locked on mine.

Chapter Fifteen

Sandy hauls up the money bag after the last of the audience has left. "I'm pretty sure we don't need to count this to know that you're in."

They hand me my share and walk away, arm in arm. I feel like my knees are about to give out, but I turn and walk the few steps to Tate.

"I heard there was a fire-breathing act in town." His voice is icy.

"I was planning to pay you back for the torches."

"I had to cancel this festival, Ally. I was going to make some serious money here."

He takes a step toward me, and I glance around the park. It's empty now, and dark.

"Please, Tate. I was desperate. I didn't have any money or anywhere else to go." I back up a step.

"Give me back my torches, Ally. And the money you made tonight."

He doesn't need the torches now. He doesn't even have a spot at the festival anymore. And there's no way I can get my hands on torches of my own for the rest of the week.

"Tate. Let me...let me rent your torches. Just let me use them for this festival. I'll give you two hundred dollars right now."

Tate looks at his bag, and then he looks at me.

"Why should I trust you?"

Why should he? I need to find something he can hold on to so he knows I'll give the torches back. I reach down and open my backpack. My hand hits the cardboard box of ashes. I pull it out slowly. There's nothing else.

"Here. Remember how I told you my mom died? These are her ashes. Hold on to them." I brush some lint off the top of the box and hand it over. "Meet me at the end of the week. I'll have your torches and give you another two hundred dollars."

Tate takes the box and reads the small typed label. I can tell he's softening.

"All right. I'll collect after the final show, but I want half of what you make this week."

"Deal." I lift his bag in a half salute.

He taps his hand on the side of the box and starts to walk away. Then he stops and turns. "Your act was good, Ally. You were great. I mean it."

I'm packing up my supplies after our last midmorning show, and Lorna is off getting ice cream. She has a long-standing claim that the quickest way to replenish after an act is through ice cream. Both Sandy and I are dubious, so Lorna has taken it as a personal challenge to convince us. The ice-cream store is just across the street, but the heat today makes walking any distance with ice cream just about impossible. As Lorna hurries across the street, melted chocolate runs down her forearms in little rivulets. She thrusts a wobbly cone at me.

"Here, it's on me."

Sandy laughs, takes her cone and licks the chocolate off Lorna. "You're not kidding, it's on you."

Lorna blushes. It's funny—despite her strong-woman persona, Lorna blushes at the drop of a hat. Sandy is always teasing her, doing stuff like licking the chocolate off her arms. I think she does it just to see Lorna, a mass of muscle, blush like a six-year-old.

I eat my soupy ice cream and let the sun sink into my bones. Only a few more shows to go, and then we're done. I should be thinking of the fat roll of money I have in the bottom of my backpack. Even with half of it earmarked for Tate, it's more than I've ever had. But all I can think of is being alone. Again.

Sandy pops the last of her ice cream into her mouth and reaches for the sunscreen. She shakes the bottle at Lorna. "Oil me up, won't you, sunshine?"

Lorna gestures to her half-eaten cone. "Get Ally to do it. I'm the only one here who doesn't eat like a starving wolf."

Sandy hands me the bottle, with instructions to get under the straps. I squirt out a dollop and smear it on her shoulders. Her skin is bumpy with star-shaped scars that rise up all over her back.

"How did you get all these scars? Is it your job or the act?"

Sandy laughs. "Running a yoga studio is pretty safe, thank God."

Lorna pats Sandy on the leg and pushes Sandy's skirt slightly higher. There is a pattern of stars all over Sandy's upper thighs as well.

"Sandy's mom liked to use her as an ashtray."

"Oh." I rub the lotion in, taking care to go under her straps. The scars are soft and pale, like baby skin. I can't stop the words. "Were you ever in the system?"

Sandy cranes her neck to look at me. "What, like foster kids and courts and stuff? Nah. I had an aunt who took me in. My mother did some time though. Apparently." She pauses and straightens her skirt. "That's the beauty of disowning someone. You don't have to care anymore."

Lorna grabs the leftover napkins and scrunches them into a ball. "Well. That was a cheery talk. We need to practice the finale again, ladies. We've got the closing show, and if we can actually pull this off, the take will be so worth it." Lorna pauses and grins at me. "Besides, I want to know if this crazy kid's ideas will work."

We get up. Lorna grabs the bags and walks ahead to our practice spot. Sandy walks beside me and gives me a little poke.

"So. You said you were going to university this fall?"

"Yeah."

"What university again?"

Shit. I can't remember what I told her last time. Something out east.

"The University of Newfoundland."

Sandy nods and looks away.

The Grand Finale event is crazy. It looks like the whole town has shown up on the beach to see the final acts perform in the glimmering twilight evening. So far, the crowd has been awesome. I feel like I can measure the dollars we're going to get by the size of their gasps and drawn-out *ooohs*. We've been practicing this finale every spare minute for the last week, but conditions haven't been good enough for us to do it in an actual performance. Now, Lorna drops Sandy down from their position and they both look at me, hoping I'll give them the thumbs-up for our big trick.

I flash my thumb, then grab the flask of fuel and my torch.

The breeze is light tonight. Lorna boosts me up to her shoulders, and I feel a ruffle of wind pick up my hair and blow it to the left. I lean onto Lorna's left shoulder. She shifts slightly, pointing me in the right direction. I tip the fuel into my mouth, tasting oil and saying a small prayer that the fire doesn't blow back into my face.

Sandy grabs the money bag and gives it a little shake. "Don't worry, folks, we're professionals. That's why we perform on the street!"

I get into position and light the torch. I lift my right leg and place both feet in Lorna's outstretched left hand. She lifts me slowly with one hand, raising me above her head. Even though she is as solid as they come, I can still feel the tiny movements in her arm as I'm lifted six feet into the air. I concentrate on my balance, on breathing without tipping forward or backward.

The crowd waits with bated breath. I lift the torch and hold it at an angle, then spray a long, even breath into the fire.

Standing on Lorna's outstretched arm, I'm already more than eleven feet tall, and with the torch angled up, the fire shoots a good twenty-five feet up into the air. A fireball leaps up into the sky like a demon and seems to pause for a moment, suspended, until the rest of the column of fire catches up to it. Orange flames arc out of my mouth like a shooting star, making the night sky a wall of flame. For a moment, even the stars disappear behind the blinding light. My body quakes with it. I am fire.

Chapter Sixteen

My bags are packed for my last lunch with Lorna and Sandy. The festival is over, and they have other circuits to visit this summer. Besides, they drive a Smart car, so I couldn't come along even if they wanted me to.

I met up with Tate after the last show and gave him back his torches as well as half the money. The rest of it is all divided up again—bills in my socks, bra, pockets, backpack and just about anywhere else I could think of. I figure if I get mugged on the road, they'll have to invest forty-five minutes in searching to get it all.

When I get to the pizza place, Lorna and Sandy are already there. They've ordered a large, and each third has a different topping group.

I can't help but laugh at my third. "We know each other too well if you're ordering tomatoes, pineapple and onion for me."

Lorna grins. "Especially since onions are disgusting. You're lucky they agreed to put your slices far away from my slices."

As we eat, all I can think about is how I'll never see them again. They think I'm this totally different person, this normal kid with a made-up mom and dad and a place to go. I think about

Lorna lifting me over her head, and about Sandy trusting me enough to throw a flaming torch into her hand.

There are only so many people in this world you can entrust with your life.

Sandy finishes her pizza and smiles at me. "I'll bet your mom is going to be glad to have you back for the rest of the summer."

I clear my throat. "About that..." I reach back and open my pack to take out my cardboard box. "I have something to tell you guys." The box is darker in the places it got wet by accident, and the label is starting to peel off the top. I set it on the table gently. "This is my mom."

Lorna draws in a breath and looks at Sandy. Sandy reaches over and takes my hand.

"Ally, honey, what the hell?"

I tell them everything, about Mom stepping in front of a bus, the foster home, Tate. Even the bit about eating out of the garbage. Lorna shakes her head, and Sandy sits back, thoughtful.

"What are you going to do now?" asks Lorna.

"She's a runaway, Lorna. She'll need to go back and report herself."

I shrug. I know it already. I can't spend the rest of my life on the street, trying to get enough money to stay in a crappy motel. At least if I go back, I'll have some money to show for the summer. When I'm eighteen, I can figure something out. Maybe work tables and busk on the side for some extra cash.

"I'll go back in a couple of days. I just need to clear my head and figure out what I'm going to say to the social worker and Darla, my foster parent."

Lorna shakes her head. "So you're really fifteen?"

"I am."

"And you have no one. No aunts or a family friend?"

Sandy takes Lorna's hand. "That's the way it is sometimes, babe."

I look at Lorna and Sandy. "There's no one. No one but you guys."

There's been an idea brewing in my head for the last few days, but I don't know if I'm crazy for even thinking it. I probably am crazy, but that's the least of my worries. I take a breath and throw it out there. "You mentioned before that you have a spare room."

Sandy shakes her head. "Ally, it's a tiny room, and we can't just take you. These things have to be legal."

"No, you can't just take me. But you can foster me. It'll give you a bit of extra cash, and there's no commitment. I mean, I could even work part-time in your yoga studio."

Lorna sets both her palms down on the table. "Ally, we need a bit of time. This has all hit me a bit out of left field.

I mean, a relationship is built on trust, and you've just come clean off of a pretty big lie."

Sandy takes my hand and gives it a squeeze. I feel my heart sink. It was stupid, but at least now they know who I am. At least someone does.

Lorna takes Sandy's other hand. "Let's meet up at our practice spot at six. I can't tell you we'll have an answer, but maybe we can talk about this a little more."

They get up to leave, and then Lorna pauses and comes back to the table. "Ally, there's one thing about your story…"

"I swear to God, Lorna, I'm telling you the truth now."

She rubs her face. "No, I know. It just occurred to me though—I think you're wrong about your mom. I don't think she committed suicide."

"What are you talking about?"

"It's just that…who packs a lunch when they're planning on jumping in front of the 9:00 AM bus?"

I sit back, stunned. I can picture it too, the way she pulled the butter knife out of the mustard jar to wave goodbye with one hand. She didn't know. Neither of us knew what was coming.

Waiting to find out about your life is a hard thing to do. The park seems empty now without all the crowds and buskers wandering around. There are only a few families now, centered on the playground. I sit down and start to pull out blades of grass, one by one.

When I spot Lorna and Sandy, I wish I could read their decision by their walks, but they're like they always are—Sandy's a graceful float, Lorna's a purposeful stride.

They sit down opposite me. Whatever happens, I had this summer on my own. And now I can choose where to go from here.

Sandy starts. "We've talked it over and called a few people. We're not really cut out to be moms, at least not yet, but if you want a place to stay, and you want to be with us, I think we can make this work."

"You'll foster me?"

Lorna takes my hand. "We'll foster you."

I reach out, and they both envelop me in a hug. We must look funny, three women hugging on the grass, Lorna's muscles bulging as she wraps her arms around me. I don't care though.

Sandy pulls back and grins at me. "There are ground rules though."

Lorna nods. "Right. Like no fire breathing inside."

I laugh. "I think I can manage that."

Epilogue

Sandy passes me the popcorn. "Did you talk to Rachel today?"

"Yeah, she's doing well. Failed her French class again though, so she's in summer school this year and pissed about it."

Lorna leans back in her chair and raises her eyebrows at Sandy "You're sure this will be better than TV?"

Sandy punches Lorna lightly. "You're dead inside if you don't like shooting stars. Everyone likes shooting stars."

I munch on the buttery popcorn and lean my head back. Mom would have liked today. It's cool on the roof of the yoga studio, and the air feels extra clean since it rained yesterday. The sky is blue-black. There's supposed to be a whole bunch of bright shooting stars tonight. Heaven's fire show.

For now, though, I'm happy just watching the familiar constellations reveal themselves piece by piece. Every star stepping into its own place in the sky.

Sarah Yi-Mei Tsiang is the author of the poetry collections *Sweet Devilry* (winner of the Gerald Lampert Award) and *Status Update*. She is also the author of four children's books and the editor of *Desperately Seeking Susans*. Sarah's work has been published and translated internationally and named to the OLA Best Bets for Children 2010, Best Books for Kids and Teens 2011 and 2012 and the Toronto Public Library's First and Best Books List (2012). She can hardly light a match without burning herself.